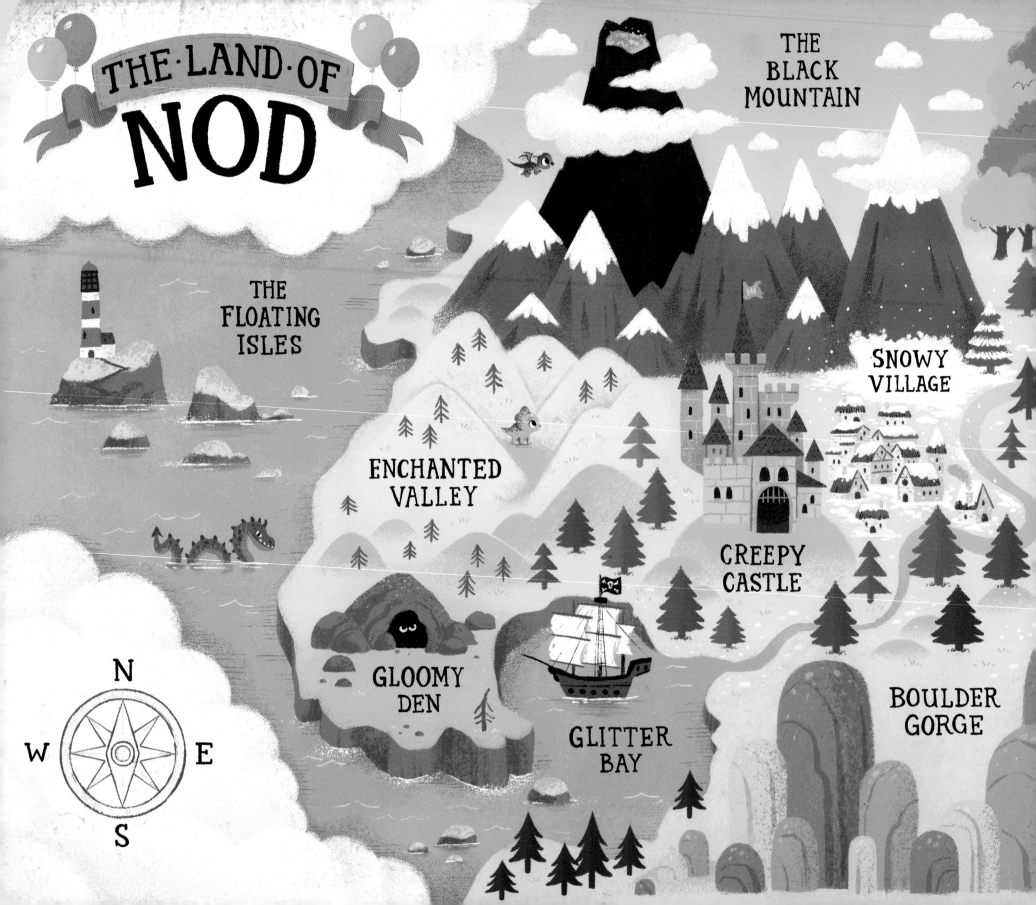

For Sue and Duncan, who hosted
so many birthday parties
R.F.

For the kind and very patient Meg
C.C.

LADYBIRD BOOKS

UK | USA | Canada | Ireland | Australia | India | New Zealand | South Africa
Ladybird Books is part of the Penguin Random House group of companies
whose addresses can be found at global.penguinrandomhouse.com.
www.penguin.co.uk   www.puffin.co.uk   www.ladybird.co.uk

Penguin
Random House
UK

First published 2020
001
Written by Rhiannon Fielding. Text copyright © Ladybird Books Ltd, 2020
Illustrations copyright © Chris Chatterton, 2020
Moral rights asserted
Printed in China
A CIP catalogue record for this book is available from the British Library
ISBN: 978–0–241–45316–2
All correspondence to:
Penguin Random House Children's
One Embassy Gardens, 8 Viaduct Gardens
London SW11 7BW

TEN MINUTES TO BED

Little Unicorn's Birthday

Rhiannon Fielding · Chris Chatterton

HAPPY BI

In a **magical glade** that was full of balloons,

gnomes rushed about, singing fun party tunes.

A banner stood tall: HAPPY BIRTHDAY! it said.

"Where's Twinkle?
It's only ten minutes to bed!"

Twinkle the unicorn ran through the wood,
jumping and leaping as high as she could.
"Nine minutes to bed!" called her dad,
strong and hearty –

for Twinkle was having a
sleepover party!

From mountains
and grottos,

from seas
and from skies,

her friends had all come
to her **birthday surprise!**

"Eight minutes to bed!"

Twinkle heard Dad exclaim,

as they all raced around
in a loud party game.

Deep in the forest,

they played **hide-and-seek**:

Dad counted down, taking care not to peek.

"**Seven minutes to bed . . .**

coming, ready or not!"

But poor
Belch the monster
was easy to spot!

While Twinkle was **prancing** and **larking** around,

she **spotted some gifts** in a pile on the ground.

With **six minutes to bedtime,**

Dad gave them to Twink –

"Happy Birthday," he said, with a smile and a wink.

Soon, Twinkle's tummy was starting to grumble,

so – followed at once by her hungry friend Rumble –

they all gathered round for a grand **birthday feast!**

(But still with **five minutes to bedtime,** at least.)

Off on a treasure hunt: 3, 2, 1,

GO!

Four minutes to bed,

so they mustn't be slow!

Splash found it first:

a big, shiny balloon

that bobbed up and down like a small, silver moon.

As Twinkle returned, something lit up the night:
a huge birthday cake,
with its candles so bright!
"Happy Birthday to you!
Make a wish," her dad said . . .

and a **colourful rainbow**
appeared overhead.

Soon, Twinkle heard a loud BANG from up high:
showers of fireworks lit up the sky!
Flicker the dragon had put on a show –

with three minutes to bedtime,
**the world seemed
to glow.**

Tucked up at last,
it was time for a story –
they lay down and listened,
all stretching and yawning.

"Two minutes to bed,"

her dad said, as he kissed her –

"Thanks for the party,"
she said in a whisper.

Under the stars, the friends
snuggled up tight,
Feeling cosy and warm
in the soft inky night.

"One minute," said dad,

"and it's my bedtime soon . . ."

. . . but **each one** was fast asleep,
under the moon.

Look out for more bedtime adventures in

THE·LAND·OF
NOD

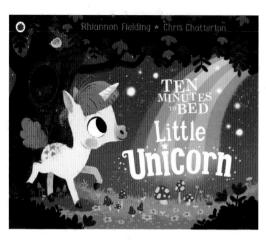
Rhiannon Fielding ★ Chris Chatterton
TEN MINUTES TO BED
Little Unicorn

Rhiannon Fielding ★ Chris Chatterton
TEN MINUTES TO BED
Little Unicorn's Christmas

Rhiannon Fielding ★ Chris Chatterton
TEN MINUTES TO BED
Little Monster

TEN MINUTES TO BED
Little Mermaid

Have you met Twinkle the unicorn, Belch the monster, Splash the mermaid and Rumble the dinosaur?

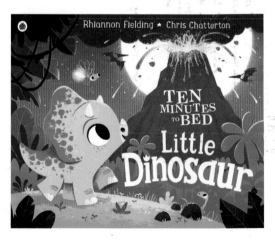
Rhiannon Fielding ★ Chris Chatterton
TEN MINUTES TO BED
Little Dinosaur

TWINKLE